GW00866323

The En Beach Hut

By

Suzanne King

Cover art and internal illustrations by
Eustace K.

Edited by
Veronica Castle

Published by
Crimson Cloak Publishing
All Rights Reserved

ISBN 13: 978-1-68160-170-0
ISBN 10: 1-68160-170-2

Publishers Publication in Data

King, Suzanne
Enchanted Beach Hut, The
1. Juvenile Fiction 2. Illustrated 3. Fantasy
4. Seaside

Table of Contents

Foreword by **Lady Leicester**:

Suzanne writes with a charming lightness of touch and introduces us to her heroine Emmeline, a feisty little girl who has her own travelling beach hut. We hear about her adventures when she comes to Norfolk, to visit her invalid cousin Alice and her strict aunt Adna.

Alice is tempted out of her sick room by Emmeline and the journeys they have in the beach hut, which takes them off to more magical places. They meet all sorts of talking animals including mice, lobsters, starfish and of course Emmeline's much loved cat, Chesterpuss, who is most concerned about his unsatisfying diet when staying at aunt Adna's.

The beach hut adventures help Alice regain her bloom and return to full health and the book concludes with a sense of promise and cheer for the future of all the main characters.

The beaches in Norfolk are particularly wild and beautiful and I was delighted to read such a captivating children's story based around them. My daughter Bess, who is 10, loved it as much as I did.

-Polly Leicester

Chapter 1
The Enchanted Beach Hut

It was the windiest day of the summer so far. The sand whipped up into the air and Emmeline covered her eyes as she made her way across the sand to the beach hut.

Emmeline loved her beach hut. It was her own place, her escape, her secret world. The wind blew Emmeline's long red hair across her face, so she scraped it back and tucked it behind her ears. She glanced at her watch and saw it was nearly 5 o'clock. She didn't have long before she had to return to 3 Chapel Road, London.

"Chesterpuss!" shouted Emmeline. Chesterpuss was Emmeline's cat, and a rather rude and stubborn cat, full of high and mighty ideas.

"Chesterpuss!" Emmeline began to panic. "Where are you?" The wind carried her voice across the sand.

Emmeline ran over to the rocks down by the sea and sure enough, there was a rustling sound and she heard the familiar tones of Chesterpuss. She peered around a rock and there he was, having a heated conversation with a very large lobster. The lobster had big pincers and was waving them about in front of Chesterpuss.

Chesterpuss was a grand-looking white cat with an equally grand black nose. He'd been sleeping while Emmeline was dipping her toes in the sea, and had been suddenly woken by a whack on the nose.

"This is my patch and my rock," shouted a very angry-looking lobster.

"I will sleep wherever I want to. This is not your beach – this beach is for everyone." Chesterpuss swiped at the lobster with his big hairy paw.

Emmeline stepped in. "I'm so sorry about my very rude friend," she said to the lobster. She glared at Chesterpuss.

"I wish you'd leave me to fight my own battles," said Chesterpuss, puffing out his chest.

"We don't have time for battles; we need to get back to the beach hut, otherwise we'll be stuck here for another day," Emmeline said firmly.

Chesterpuss turned his back, pointed his tail in the air and flicked it at the lobster.

"I'm sorry, Mr Lobster," Emmeline apologised again.

"No need to apologise for the rude cat," said the lobster.

Emmeline smiled and, slightly embarrassed, waved goodbye to the lobster. She caught up with Chesterpuss and they made their way back to the beach hut.

The beach hut was a pretty little hut: green and white, with two steps leading up to the door. Once inside, Emmeline sat down on the wicker chair, emptied her pockets, which were full of shells, and placed them on top of her bookshelf. She had collected many objects on her travels, which she proudly displayed on the shelves and on the little boat-shaped bookcase.

Chesterpuss sat on his cushion in the corner and licked his feet, trying to get all the sand out from in between his toes.

"Tuna and porridge for tea," Emmeline said, trying to get his attention.

"Let me sulk," he replied, though he raised his eyebrows at the thought of tuna and porridge.

Emmeline turned to the wall, pointed to London on the map of England and pressed down hard. "Hold tight!" she said.

Chesterpuss gripped his cushion with his sharp claws.

Whoosh! Whoosh! Whizz! The little beach hut began to lift and the wind rushed around it as it rose higher and higher into the sky. Emmeline clung to her chair and Chesterpuss scooted across the floor on his cushion, his eyes wide as tennis balls. The hut shook and the shutters on the window banged back and forth. The shells and books fell from the bookshelf, landing on top of Chesterpuss.

The noise was so loud that Emmeline covered her ears ... and then came an almighty thud. The beach hut had landed and

Chesterpuss was now squashed in the corner, upside-down, with a pile of books on top of him.

Emmeline gave a sigh of relief. They had landed safely back home, in the garden of 3, Chapel Road, London.

Chapter 2
Going Away

A few weeks later

Winter was coming to an end, the trees were bare and the fields looked flat and empty. From the train, Emmeline could just make out the sign in the station and an old man ringing a hand-bell as he walked along the platform, shouting, "Skipwick Station – next stop Blakeney."

Emmeline had to get off otherwise the train would start to move. She jumped down onto the platform with her suitcase. It felt cold out there after the warmth on the train, so she pulled her scarf around her neck, picked up her suitcase and smiled at the old man ringing the bell.

Something was missing – yes, it was Chesterpuss. "Where is he?" whispered Emmeline.

"Are you looking for this, Miss?" came a reply from behind her.

There in the arms of the porter, was Chesterpuss.

"Thank you, sir," said Emmeline, taking Chesterpuss and tucking him under her arm.

"Stand back, Miss, please," said the porter. "The train is about to set off; please step away from the railway line." He waved his flag.

Emmeline covered her ears as the high-pitched shriek of the porter's whistle made them hurt. The train moved slowly away and Emmeline plonked herself down on the nearest bench. She had been given strict instructions not to leave the station but to wait for her lift.

Two women and their children were standing near the platform on the other side of the railway line. They had brown long coats and matching hats; the children wearing the same clothing as the adults. In fact everywhere Emmeline looked, the people wore similar clothes – very brown, thought Emmeline, unlike her own green velvet coat.

Emmeline came from an affluent background and was lucky to have lots of bright clothing. Often her father would bring her back clothes from his travels around the world. Emmeline was going to miss her father, as he wasn't due back from overseas until the end of the summer.

She had been sent to stay with her cousin Alice and strict Aunt Adna. It was a few years since she had last seen Alice, who was kept inside all the time, as Aunt Adna was afraid she would pick up germs and become very ill. Aunt Adna and Emmeline's mum were sisters, unfortunately Emmeline's mum passed away when Emmeline was 5 years old, she left her daughter the beach hut in her will. In the beach hut, there had been a note left and it said, "Wherever you travel, I will be with you".

Emmeline's father had promised he would have her beach hut delivered to Aunt Adna's. Emmeline couldn't wait to see it again. Aunt Adna had been against the idea of a beach hut in her garden, but Emmeline's father had managed to talk her round.

"As long as it's tucked away at the bottom of the garden where I can't see it," Aunt Adna had said in her spiky manner.

Honk, honk. A car horn sounded, making Emmeline jump.

She peered over the wall and saw a tall man, jumping up and down and waving a sign. Emmeline could just make out what it said. TAXI FOR EMMELINE.

Chesterpuss, who had been rubbing around her legs, made a sudden dash towards the car. The man opened the door and Chesterpuss jumped in. Emmeline took this to be her lift to her aunt's house.

The man smiled, took Emmeline's suitcase and placed it in the back of the car. "Good journey, Emmeline?" he asked.

"Yes, thank you," said Emmeline.

"I see you have your cat with you. What's his name?" The man stroked Chesterpuss.

"His name is Chesterpuss," said Emmeline.

Chesterpuss pushed his head away from the man.

"Well, my name is Mr James," the man said, attempting to stroke Chesterpuss again.

Emmeline smiled and settled herself down, ready for the journey. In spite of the cold, she was interested in this new county, with its flat fields and small stone buildings – very different to the busy city of London. As the car drove out of the train station and onto the windy roads, Emmeline looked across the fields – flat as far as you could see. In the distance, she could make out a cluster of stone buildings and a church. *What a wonderful place*, she thought to herself. Every door and every little picket gate was painted bottle green – they all looked so pretty against the stone brickwork.

Chesterpuss tapped her on the shoulder, waking her from a daydream. "Is it far?|"

Chesterpuss sniffed Emmeline's hair, which made her giggle. "Just a few miles down the road," she whispered.

Mr James was concentrating on the road and occasionally honking his horn at familiar faces. The car started to slow down and Emmeline looked out to see a beautiful stone house with a walled garden and its own bottle green picket gate.

"Looks lovely," she said.

Mr James smiled at her. "Come on, your aunt will be expecting us and we wouldn't want her getting into one of her spiky moods."

Chesterpuss and Emmeline stepped out of the car and Mr James gathered up Emmeline's belongings. Emmeline followed him through the garden. It looked so tired and drab – a bit like an unloved garden. What it needed was a beach hut and pretty flowers, thought Emmeline – it just looked so sad.

Mr James had gone ahead and disappeared into the house, with Chesterpuss close on his heels, meowing as he went. Emmeline pushed the door open, noticed the temperature had dropped dramatically and pulled her scarf around her neck. "Gosh, this place is so cold," she whispered to herself as she walked along the hallway.

"Hello," she called out.

There wasn't a sound in the house and Chesterpuss and Mr James were nowhere to be seen. As Emmeline made her way down the long hallway she saw a big door with a stained glass window, through which she glimpsed the flickering of flames.

She turned the handle and was greeted by a blazing fire. Sitting on the settle by the fire, looking at a book, which she closed and put into her pocket as Emmeline walked in, was Aunt Adna.

Chapter 3
Aunt Adna

Aunt Adna was tall, elegant and kind of beautiful, but she had the stern look of an ice queen. She had white, peppery hair which was cut in a short, sharp style, and her red lipstick made her teeth look perfectly white. *If only she smiled, she would be so pretty*, thought Emmeline.

There were no hugs or greetings. Aunt Adna went straight in with the house rules. "Emmeline, I expect you to help out Nancy with the housework from time to time." Nancy was the housemaid/cook/dogsbody.

"And I don't want you bothering your cousin and getting her too excited," Aunt Adna continued. "You will have half an hour a day with Alice and no longer." She narrowed her eyes and looked down at her feet.

Chesterpuss had found Emmeline and was now rubbing himself around Aunt Adna's ankles.

"What's that?" Aunt Adna shrieked.

"That's my cat, Chesterpuss," said Emmeline, quickly gathering Chesterpuss up in her arms.

"The cat will stay out of the bedrooms and be restricted to the kitchen," said Aunt Adna sternly.

"Suits me," whispered Chesterpuss.

"Sshhh," said Emmeline, trying to cover her cat's mouth.

"Did you say something?" Aunt Adna leaned in towards Emmeline and narrowed her eyes at Chesterpuss.

"Er, no, Aunt ... I just have a sniffle." Emmeline pulled her hanky out of her pocket.

"Then keep that thing away from Alice. Under no circumstances shall it go anywhere near my daughter." Aunt Adna rang a little bell and Nancy came running to attention.

"Please take that awful animal out of here," Aunt Adna said. "And can you serve some tea and cakes, please?"

Nancy gathered a disgruntled Chesterpuss in her arms and rushed off to get the tea.

Emmeline looked around the room, with its long, heavy, dusty curtains and big furniture. A grandfather clock stood in the corner, proud and tall. Emmeline caught something out of the corner of her eye – a little mouse dressed in red, sitting on top of the clock. In an instant he was gone again. Had she really seen him, or was she just tired?

The door opened and in walked Nancy with her little trolley, a teapot, cups and jam tarts. "It's mighty cold out there today. Would you like a cup of tea to warm you up?" she said to Emmeline.

She gave Emmeline a jam tart and Emmeline gobbled it up. It was delicious; she had never tasted a jam tart like it before.

"Would you like another one, Emmeline?" said Nancy, passing her a second tart.

"Not too many," said Aunt Adna. "It will spoil her dinner." She took the second jam tart from Emmeline and ate it herself, leaving a blob of jam on her cheek. Emmeline fixed her eyes upon the blob of jam which moved up and down as Aunt Adna spoke.

Nancy raised her eyebrows, gave Emmeline a little smile and mouthed, "I'll save you some."

Emmeline saw that Nancy was going to be someone she could talk to. Aunt Adna clearly wasn't the talking type; she was cold, unlike Nancy, who had a lovely warm feel about her.

"Can you ask Mr James to take Emmeline's suitcase up to the pink room?" said Aunt Adna.

Nancy left the room with the trolley and went to find Mr James. She found him lying on the sofa sprawled on his back with his mouth wide open, snoring loudly. Nancy pinched his nose and Mr James caught his breath and sat up, startled.

"What have I missed?" he blurted out in a snorting sort of way.

"Nothing, you have missed nothing" said Nancy, laughing.

"Lady Adna would like you to take Emmeline's suitcase up to the pink bedroom," Nancy said, still laughing. "Don't let her catch you falling asleep."

Nancy liked to tease Mr James, and deep down he secretly enjoyed the attention. He picked up Emmeline's suitcase and did as he was told. He was very fond of Nancy and would do anything to stay in her good books.

Chapter 4
Chesterpuss

Chesterpuss was sitting in a corner of the kitchen, preening himself and occasionally looking up at the banging of saucepans and plates. Nancy was preparing dinner, which was always at 6pm sharp.

Nancy loved cooking and she liked to nibble while she worked, which contributed to her rather round, full figure.

Back from taking the suitcase upstairs, Mr James fussed around Nancy, whistling, jumping up and down and getting in her way.

"Do something useful and feed that cat," Nancy said.

"Time for tea, is it, cat?" Mr James called out.

Chesterpuss looked up in anticipation, hoping for his favourite tuna and porridge, but

Mr James plonked a small bowl of dry-looking biscuits in front of him. Chesterpuss wasn't impressed. Disgruntled, he crouched down to eat his tea. He couldn't afford to cause any fuss on his first day, but he made a mental note to discuss the menu with Emmeline.

In the middle of the kitchen was a big, imposing wooden table with lots of pots and pans on it. Nancy always said you couldn't have too many saucepans. There were more of them on the shelves attached to the wall.

On one side of the wall was a line of bells – one for each room in the house. The large pantry led off the kitchen and was full of yummy things to eat. As in most pantries, there was a meat store where the meat was left to keep cool. Tins of fruit were stacked on the shelves and big blocks of cheese stood on top of each other.

The pantry was going to be Chesterpuss's favourite room.

Nancy had already chased him out with a broom – but as you can imagine, he was going to chance it again, with all that cheese in there.

Chesterpuss licked his lips. Mr James picked up his bowl, which was completely empty. Unfortunately he stood on Chesterpuss's tail.

"Meoooowwwww! You nincompoop – watch where you're stepping!"

Mr James stood back in shock. "What did you call me?" he asked.

"I called you a nincompoop," said Chesterpuss.

"A talking cat," gasped Mr James. "I'm not a nincompoop," he added, bending down to get a closer look at Chesterpuss.

"You are, and you have very large feet," said Chesterpuss. "And can you please close that rather large mouth of yours – I don't want to see your tonsils," he added sternly.

"You really can speak," said Mr James, laughing.

"Yes, I really can. Get used to it, let it sink in – I can speak." Chesterpuss blinked and moved his head away, as Mr James was now far too close to him. "Do something useful and fill my bowl with cream, and we will say no more about this standing on the tail business."

It was from this day on that Mr James and Chesterpuss had a sort of mutual understanding. Mr James filled the cat's bowl with cream and Chesterpuss rubbed around his ankles; that was his way of thanking Mr James.

"Mr James," came a call from Nancy. "Please can you nip to the corner shop to get some groceries?"

Mr James came running and took a bag from Nancy. "That cat talks – keep an eye on it, Nancy, you never know what it will do next." Mr James toddled off to the shop, shaking his head as he went.

Nancy continued with the dinner, thinking Mr James was losing his marbles. As she reached up to get one of the saucepans, she saw something move out the corner of her eye. A mouse!

"Arghhhhh!" she screamed.

Chesterpuss looked up from drinking his cream, and his big green eyes widened. The mouse leaped from the shelf across the top of the copper saucepans and made a dash for the pantry.

"Stop him!" shouted Nancy.

Chesterpuss dived for the mouse.

"Grab it," Nancy yelled.

The mouse was just too quick for Chesterpuss and ran under the gap in the pantry door. Chesterpuss flew like a bird across the kitchen and landed on the door handle. The door burst open and Chesterpuss jumped onto the shelf. Boxes of tea and coffee and packets of flour tumbled to the floor. It was complete mayhem.

Mr James had not quite reached the front door. When he heard all the commotion, he dashed back into the kitchen. Nancy was standing on the table, pointing to the broom in the corner of the room.

"Just get him out, the mouse – get him out," she yelled at Mr James.

Meanwhile, in the pantry, Chesterpuss had given up on the mouse and was tucking in to some pongy cheese.

"You're too late," Chesterpuss said to Mr James, between mouthfuls. "He went that way." Pointing to a hole in the skirting board, Chesterpuss grinned a big cat grin at Mr James.

"Get out of the pantry now," said Mr James, in a very quiet but stern voice.

Chesterpuss, sensing Mr James wasn't happy, popped one more bit of cheese into his mouth and made a quick exit. Mr James cleaned the mess up and explained to Nancy that he had chased the mouse out into the garden.

Chesterpuss felt very full and happy – he loved pongy cheese.

Suddenly a bell started to ring. Nancy looked up and saw it was number 8, which was the one for Alice's room.

"Mr James, Mr James, I have to go, please clean the kitchen up," Nancy cried. "I'm needed – it's young Alice."

Chesterpuss's ears pricked up. *Alice, did they say?* Chesterpuss made a dash for the door, but Mr James got there first and shut it straight in Chesterpuss's face. *Was he ever going to meet Alice?*

Chapter 5
Alice

"**A**unt, can I come up and see Alice?" Emmeline asked nervously.

"You can, but only for half an hour" said her aunt. "Nancy will be giving her some tablets before dinner. And tomorrow, Emmeline, I have a few errands to run, would you like to accompany me? Or if you wish, you can stay and explore the house." Adna opened the door to Alice's room.

"I will stay, Aunt, thank you," said Emmeline, eager to see Alice.

The room was dark, with just a small amount of light shining in between the curtains. Emmeline hugged her cousin, who looked awfully pale and weak.

"Hello, Emmeline," said Alice excitedly.

Nancy was already in the room, counting out the tablets.

"What are the tablets for?" enquired Emmeline.

"They are her vitamin pills," said Aunt Adna. "Why are you so inquisitive, child?"

Alice was happy to see someone of her own age. She liked Emmeline a lot. The girls hugged each other, but Aunt Adna separated them. "Hurry along and get ready for dinner," she said to Emmeline.

"I'll come and see you tomorrow," whispered Emmeline in Alice's ear.

"Promise?" said Alice.

"Promise," answered Emmeline.

Alice smiled and waved goodbye to her cousin. She swallowed her vitamins and Aunt Adna tucked her sheets back in so everything was neat and tidy.

Aunt Adna didn't like Alice having visitors. She believed that Alice had a very weak immune system. Poor Alice had once suffered with pneumonia and, from the day she got better, Aunt Adna had kept her away from everyone, in sterile conditions, so she would never be ill again.

Alice was very pale – almost ghostly-looking, even down to the gown she wore, which was crisp and white like her bed sheets.

It was almost like being a prisoner, thought Emmeline. She had to get her cousin out of that room somehow, and she desperately wanted to show her the travelling beach hut. That was it – she had to travel with Alice. That way, she knew Alice would get better.

It was just a question of how she was going to do it, without Aunt Adna finding out.

Chapter 6
The Arrival

After breakfast, Emmeline said goodbye to her aunt and watched her walk down the road out of sight. As Aunt Adna turned the corner, a large lorry pulled into the street. Yes, it was Emmeline's beach hut.

"It's here!" Emmeline set off at a run, her feet hardly touching the ground. She burst into the kitchen. "It's here, Mr James, it's here." She tugged on Mr James's coat.

"I'm coming," Mr James said, making his way out into the garden to help the men with the beach hut.

Emmeline waited in anticipation as they lowered it into place, through the rose-covered arch at the bottom end of the garden – just where Aunt Adna had instructed.

"Left a bit, right, right ..." shouted Mr James to the lorry driver.

Eventually, down it came. Emmeline clapped her hands.

"Thank you," said Mr James to the men, and they drove off.

"'Well, there it is," said Mr James. "Though I personally can't see what all the fuss is about." He turned around to Emmeline, but she was already inside the hut.

"I've missed you so much." Emmeline looked around the hut, checking that everything was still in its place. The map on the wall, the cigar box and all the pine cones and shells were all still there. Emmeline looked out of the window and saw Mr James disappearing into the house.

Then it happened. The sun came out and the garden came to life. The birds began to sing and everything suddenly seemed magical. The flowers started to open and what lovely colours they were – rich reds, bright blues and delicate mauves. The little fountain in front of the hut started to bubble and a spray of silver water shot out of it.

Emmeline felt so happy, running her fingers through the water. She took off her coat, laid it on the grass and sat down. She was going to enjoy every minute, now her beach hut had arrived. She lay back on her coat and began to drift off to sleep, but she was woken by a chirpy little voice.

"You call that marching?"

Emmeline turned her head to the side and there, right next to her nose, were two little mice. She tried to focus, which made her go bog-eyed. One mouse was wearing a dress, the other one trousers and a shirt, and they were marching up and down.

"Of course it's marching. You have to bring your legs up to your chin, like this," said the little mouse in the dress, demonstrating her march.

Emmeline watched with fascination as the mice marched up and down, up and down.

"Left, right, left, right ..." Both mice were oblivious of Emmeline, watching.

'Hello,' said Emmeline.

There was a long silence. The mice froze, not daring to turn round.

"You must be frightened – don't be." Emmeline moved closer to the mice. They were like little statues, frozen by Emmeline's voice. The mouse wearing the trousers turned round very slowly to face her.

She again went bog-eyed. "I wouldn't dream of hurting you." Emmeline smiled at the mice.

The little mouse in the trousers cleared his throat and nervously spoke. "Hello."

"How wonderful!" Emmeline squealed with excitement.

"Gosh," said the little mouse in the trousers, now standing back from Emmeline. "You have very big eyes and a great big nose."

"How rude," said Emmeline.

"Please can you stop screeching – we only have very small ears," said the mouse in the dress.

"I'm so sorry, I really don't mean to scare you," said Emmeline. "I shall sit up." She sat up so that she was looking down on the mice. "Where are you going? Do you live in the garden?" she asked, feeling she might explode with excitement.

"No, we are house mice. We live under the floorboards in the pantry," said the mouse in the trousers.

"What are your names?" asked Emmeline.

"My name is Pip and this is Penelope." Pip pushed Penelope forward.

"I'm Emmeline and I'm very pleased to meet you both." Emmeline held her little finger out to shake hands with the mice.

Very reluctantly, Penelope stretched out her small hand and met Emmeline's finger.

"Would you like to see my beach hut?" said Emmeline.

Pip and Penelope looked at each other. Although still a little wary, they both wanted to see the beach hut. "Yes, we would like to look at your beach hut," said Pip.

"Then march this way." Emmeline jumped up and began to march towards the beach hut, followed by Pip and Penelope.

"It's lovely," said Penelope, looking at the pretty flags pinned around the walls.

"Thank you," said Emmeline. She sat down on her wicker chair and placed a little shell upside-down on the shelf. "Here, take a seat." She pointed to the shell.

Both mice ran up the flags and onto the shelf, where they sat down on the shells.

"See that cigar box? You can have it as a bed if you like." Emmeline opened the cigar box and placed a little handkerchief into it, and a small pin cushion for a pillow.

Pip climbed into the box, followed by Penelope.

"Thank you so much," said Penelope.

"You're welcome; you can use it anytime," said Emmeline.

The beach hut door creaked and in walked Chesterpuss. Pip and Penelope disappeared under the handkerchief and slid the cigar box shut.

Chesterpuss's ears pricked up.

"Chesterpuss, be nice." Emmeline grabbed his collar. "These mice are my new friends and I don't want you to hurt them. You have to promise me, Chesterpuss." She held on tight to his collar.

"You can let go of my collar – I'm not going to hurt them," said Chesterpuss. "Anyway, mice give me hairballs and come to think of it, I would rather eat porridge and tuna or pongy cheese." Chesterpuss began to daydream.

"Pip, Penelope, you can come out." Emmeline opened the cigar box to find two trembling little mice.

"Come and sit on my back," said Chesterpuss. "I give you my word, I will not hurt you." He turned his head and faced the door. "Come, jump on," he said.

Pip shivered. He remembered being chased through the pantry by Chesterpuss.

"I was only playing with you earlier. I wouldn't have eaten you." Chesterpuss pointed his tail so the mice could jump down onto it.

A look of fear on Pip's face made Emmeline hold the two mice close to her. She sat down and let them gradually move towards Chesterpuss. Chesterpuss came close and was now a nose-length away from the mice. Pip and Penelope could feel his breath.

"I come in peace," said Chesterpuss, bowing his head.

Emmeline giggled. "You're so funny, Chesterpuss."

"I can be funny. I'm not always grumpy."

The mice took deep breaths and stepped onto the big white fluffy cat. Penelope grabbed his long white fur, as Chesterpuss raised his head and started to walk around the beach hut.

Pip clung onto the collar around Chesterpuss's neck. Both mice swung from side to side as Chesterpuss jumped onto Emmeline's knee.

"Sometimes you surprise me," said Emmeline, stroking Chesterpuss and taking Pip and Penelope into her hand.

"Maybe now is a good time to discuss the food at this place," said Chesterpuss.

"Let me guess, there is no porridge and tuna on the menu," said Emmeline, popping Pip and Penelope back into the cigar box. "If you are a very good cat and you are kind to Penelope and Pip, then I will ask Nancy to give you your favourite tuna and porridge." She covered up Pip and Penelope in the cigar box.

Chesterpuss licked his lips at the thought of his favourite dish. "I must say, I would rather eat porridge and tuna than mice – no offence." He looked up at Penelope and Pip.

"None taken," said Pip.

"OK. Now we are all friends, I need your help," said Emmeline. "I want to fly the hut again and I want to take Alice with us. We need to sneak her out of her bedroom while Aunt Adna is away for the day."

"A flying beach hut"' Penelope said, peering over the edge of the cigar box.

"Yes, this is my travelling beach hut. Take a look around you at the walls," said Emmeline, pointing to the map on the wall of the hut.

Pip and Penelope gazed at the map, which had little markers pinned to it.

"Those little white flags are all the beaches I've visited with Chesterpuss," said Emmeline.

"Wow!" said Pip.

"My mother travelled to Paris and Egypt in this beach hut," said Emmeline. She took a book from the boat-shaped bookcase and carefully turned the pages. It was a very old book, the pages were delicate and the writing on the maps had begun to fade. Each page represented a place that had once been visited by Emmeline's mother.

Pip and Penelope listened with excitement.

"24th September 1932, St Ives, Cornwall," Emmeline read from the book. "27th June, Cardigan Bay, in Wales."

"I remember that day well," said Chesterpuss. "We met Mr Griddle, a fisherman with his boat in the bay." Chesterpuss licked his lips as he re-lived the day. "What a feast I had, fish after fish ..." He began to dream.

"Does he always daydream like that?" Penelope asked.

"Quite often," said Emmeline. "He goes into a trance."

"How old is he?" said Penelope.

"He must be very old," said Pip.

"Ancient," replied Emmeline.

"I'm still here, you know," said Chesterpuss, waking from his daydream.

Emmeline turned the pages, one after another. Pip and Penelope looked in amazement at the places Emmeline's mum had visited.

"What about this one?" said Pip, pointing to a drawing of a beautiful beach along the edge of a forest. The beach was white and there were a couple of beach huts painted in bright colours with bunting strewn across them. In the corner of the page, Emmeline's mum had drawn four characters – a lobster, a crab, a starfish and a tall man with a moon-shaped face.

"That is Holkham, my favourite place in the world," said Emmeline. "I will take you all there, if you promise to help me with Aunt Adna."

"Of course," said Pip and Penelope together.

"We will all help," said Chesterpuss, stroking his whiskers.

"Then that's a deal," said Emmeline.

As Emmeline and Chesterpuss walked across the garden, back to the house, they turned and waved to Pip and Penelope. The mice were now settled for the night in their new home, the beach hut, with their new bed, the cigar box.

Emmeline looked up to the window above the kitchen and saw what she thought was Alice in her white nightgown. Looking again, she realised it was Aunt Adna, gazing down at her in the garden.

"Mmm, I don't trust that Emmeline – she's up to something," said Aunt Adna. "I'm going to keep a close eye on her while she's here."

"You worry too much, Mother," said Alice.

"I may be wrong, but I think I'm right." Aunt Adna closed the curtains. "I will have Nancy bring up your dinner for you." She tucked Alice into her bed and left the room.

Alice waited until she couldn't hear her mother's footsteps anymore and then crept quietly out of bed and across to the window. She slowly pulled back the curtains and looked out into the garden. In the moonlight, Alice caught a glimpse of a little face with what looked like enormous ears. It was the shadow of Pip. He had stepped down onto the step of the beach hut, which was glowing very bright, like the sun.

Alice gulped and pulled back from the window. She flew across her bedroom and jumped back into bed. And there she stayed, shaking with excitement.

Chapter 7
Alice's Journey

Emmeline closed the door on the sunny garden and sat down on the little wicker chair. Chesterpuss took his place on the cushion in the corner of the beach hut. Pip and Penelope slipped out of the cigar box and sat on the shelf.

"OK. Aunt Adna is due to go to see her friend in the village today, according to Nancy, and she will be gone most of the day." Emmeline sounded like a captain lining up her troops for battle. "Chesterpuss, you stay and watch at the bottom of the garden behind the yew tree," she went on. "As soon as Aunt Adna is out of sight, you whistle and I, with the help of Nancy, will fetch Alice down from her bedroom." Pointing to the map on the wall, Emmeline smiled and said, "And then we'll wait until Nancy is back in the house and we'll fly high up into the sky and land on my favourite beach."

Aunt Adna said goodbye to Alice and the others and made her way down the path to the garden gate. She stared down at Chesterpuss, who was sitting near the yew tree. "Horrible furry white thing," she muttered as she shut the gate behind her.

Chesterpuss watched as Aunt Adna disappeared around the corner of the street. He tried to whistle, but nothing came out. He tried again – still nothing. "Oh, no," he said. "This is a complete nightmare."

"Owee!" shouted Pip. Chesterpuss looked round and saw Pip sitting next to him. "OK, I can't whistle. Nobody bothered to ask if I could whistle." He tried to put his paw into his mouth.

With that, Pip put his two little paws in his mouth and let out a long, high-pitched whistle.

"A big whistle from such a little mouse," said Chesterpuss, and had another try, but nothing came out.

Emmeline and Nancy were in the top window. Alice was dressed in warm clothes, including a huge purple bobble-hat.

"Nancy insisted," said Alice with a giggle. She hadn't been outside for over a year and Nancy couldn't take any chances.

"I've packed you a picnic to eat in the beach hut," said Nancy, passing Emmeline the basket. "You have cheese sandwiches and jam tarts, with some apple juice to wash it down."

"Thank you," said Emmeline, taking the basket.

Mr James helped Alice down the stairs, and Emmeline followed. Out in the garden, the spring sun hit Alice's face.

"The garden is so bright – and look at all the lovely flowers," Alice cried with delight.

They reached the beach hut and opened the door. Chesterpuss was already sitting on his cushion. The two mice were out of sight in the cigar box.

"Look after her," said Mr James to Emmeline. "I'll be back at 4 o'clock to collect you, Alice, before your mother gets home." Mr James shut the door of the beach hut and went off to help Nancy in the kitchen.

"So this is what you wrote to me about – you and your travelling beach hut. I was so excited last night I couldn't sleep," said Alice, who was now sitting in comfort on the wicker chair.

"Yes, it is," said Emmeline, "and I can't wait to show you the lovely beach we're going to. But first, I would like you to meet Chesterpuss." Emmeline pointed to Chesterpuss, sitting on his cushion. "And where are Pip and Penelope, my mouse friends?"

Pip and Penelope emerged from the cigar box.

"Am I dreaming?" said Alice, pinching herself.

"No, you're not dreaming, it's all true. Now, are we all ready?" Emmeline closed the door on the sunny garden and everyone braced themselves for the journey. Chesterpuss dug his nails into the cushion, knowing what to expect.

"Hold on tight," said Emmeline to Alice.

Alice held on to the wicker chair, and Pip and Penelope held tight to the cigar box.

"It could be a rough ride." Emmeline placed her finger on the map on the wall and pointed to a place called Holkham, in Norfolk.

Nothing happened – no movement, nothing. Then the cigar box shuffled across the shelf and Pip and Penelope grabbed hold of one another.

"I wish, I wish to fly, high in the sky," chanted Emmeline.

There was a long silence – and then the hut started to rock from side to side. Alice clung to the chair as the hut rose into the air.

Whoosh, whoosh ... The wind rushed around the hut, making the shutters on the window clatter as they opened and shut again. Alice's stomach felt like a washing machine, whirring round and round. The noise was tremendous – and then ...

Whizz, bang, whizz, bang ... The hut had landed.

Chesterpuss was upside-down in the corner of the beach hut. He did a roly-poly and sat up straight.

"Are you OK?" said Alice, looking concerned.

"Yes, he's fine," said Emmeline, brushing her hair away from her eyes.

"Are we here?" said Alice.

"Yes, we're here," said Chesterpuss, sniffing the sea air wafting into the hut as Emily opened the door.

Emmeline opened up the cigar box. "Hope that wasn't too bumpy for you two."

Pip and Penelope climbed down onto Chesterpuss's back. Pip's little red hat was covering his eyes, and Penelope straightened her crumpled dress.

One by one they stepped out onto the beach, Emmeline holding Alice's hand.

"This is just beautiful," said Alice. "Thank you for bringing me here." She hugged her cousin.

"This is just the beginning," said Emmeline. "I have a few friends for you to meet and we are invited for lunch." Emmeline turned to the two mice. "You are both welcome to come along," she said.

"You go and enjoy yourselves," said Pip.

"We'll wait here until you get back," said Penelope.

"As you wish," said Emmeline. "I'll see you both later."

Off they all went. Chesterpuss was already making his way across the beach. Emmeline and Alice kicked off their shoes and enjoyed the feel of the sand wiggling through their toes.

"Don't forget to be back before 4 o'clock," shouted Penelope.

Alice looked around her. The place was simply stunning, with the blue sky meeting the even bluer sea. She could taste the salt on her tongue.

"Come along, Emmeline, catch up. It's not like we have all day," said Chesterpuss.

"We're coming," said Emmeline, giggling with Alice.

"This sand is rather hard to walk on," said Alice.

Chesterpuss had reached the sea and was waiting by the rock for Emmeline and Alice. Beside the rock was a boat with paddles. Chesterpuss jumped in. "I hope I live to regret this," he mumbled to himself.

"I heard that," said Emmeline, who had now reached the boat. "You say that every time we get into the boat, and you're still here." She laughed as she helped Alice climb in.

"This is so exciting. Where are we sailing to?" said Alice.

"We're going to sail over there," said Emmeline, pointing to a very large rock. "It will bring us out on the other side, where the forest lines the edge of the beach." She picked the oars up and started to row.

"Is this the beach you wrote to me about in your letters, Emmeline?" said Alice.

"It is, and you'll love it, Alice. I'm so pleased you're here to see it." Emmeline rowed against the strong current, the sea spraying over into the little paddling boat.

"The boat is going the wrong way," shouted Chesterpuss. "Turn your oars around and row the other way," he yelled at Emmeline.

"He always panics – he hates water" said Emmeline. Eventually they were back en route and heading towards the big rock, Emmeline rowing with all her might.

The sun shone down on Alice's face and her cheeks glowed. Emmeline smiled at her cousin, very happy that she was here. As they paddled around the rock, there it was ... the pine forest. Just as Emmeline had described in her letters to Alice, it lined the white beach. The boat bobbed up and down as they hit the shoreline.

"Thank goodness for that," said Chesterpuss.

Emmeline and Alice tied the rope round a piece of wood which was sticking out of the sand.

"Ouch!" came a noise.

Alice, startled, nervously looked behind the post and saw a big red lobster. Sitting next to the lobster was a crab, and next to the crab was a starfish. Alice stared at them, her face returning to its familiar shade of white. She had never seen sea creatures as large as this before; they were the same size as Chesterpuss.

"What's the matter with you?" said the lobster, pulling his claw away from the post. Alice had accidently tied the lobster's claw to the wood.

"You look positively ill," the lobster went on.

"She looks like she needs to sit down," said the crab.

"Sit down next to me," said the starfish, who was wearing seven green gloves, one on each tentacle. "You poor thing," it added.

"I think she's maybe a little startled by you all," said Chesterpuss, making a grand appearance.

"Oh, it's you again," said the lobster, giving Chesterpuss the eye.

"She mustn't be frightened of us," said the starfish kindly.

"Now come on, you two," said Emmeline, coming to the rescue and taking Alice by the hand before she fell over. "I see you've met my friends. This is Starfish and this is Crab – and we meet again, Mr Lobster." Emmeline held out her hand to shake the lobster's claw and gave a little curtsy.

"We do," said the lobster, shaking her hand with his claw.

"May I introduce my cousin Alice?" Emmeline said.

"Hello," said Alice, the colour starting to return to her cheeks. "I must say you did rather startle me. I've never come across such large crustaceans before." She sat down, close to Emmeline.

"Well, Alice, have you ever in your life seen such a fantastic specimen as me?" said the crab.

"No, I haven't" said Alice, feeling a little more relaxed.

"Oh, don't listen to him," said the starfish. "He's always thinking about the way he looks. Now, Emmeline, would you all like to come over and have some lunch?"

"We've brought lunch with us, but there's plenty to go round," said Emmeline, producing the picnic that Nancy had prepared.

"Come on, everyone – let's make our way home up to the edge of the forest. Bring the picnic with you, Emmeline." The starfish motioned everyone to follow her as she made her way towards the pine forest.

A few minutes later, they were all walking single file across the white sand, when something caught Emmeline's eye. She could see an object moving up and down in the distance. As it got closer she squinted her eyes together and opened them again. She'd know that box anywhere – it was the cigar box. And there were Pip and Penelope, waving their little arms frantically.

"Stop!" yelled Emmeline. She turned to Chesterpuss. "Look out to sea."

Chesterpuss turned to see what all the fuss was about. "Those darn mice, and what do you expect me to do about it?" he asked.

"We have to rescue them before they drown," cried Emmeline.

"I can't get wet," said Chesterpuss.

"Get the boat," instructed Lobster.

Alice and Emmeline untied the rope from the post and threw it into the boat. They jumped in, followed by the lobster, the crab and the starfish.

Chesterpuss stood firm on the sand, while they all stared at him. "All right, all right, I'm coming," he sighed.

Emmeline picked up the oars and started to paddle as fast as her arms would allow her. The cigar box was gradually getting soggier and soggier, and Pip and Penelope were running out of steam.

"Hang on!" shouted Emmeline.

Pip's ears pricked up. He recognised Emmeline's voice – and there in front of him he saw the boat.

"Can you get a little closer?" came the request from Lobster as he positioned himself at the front of the boat.

Emmeline pulled the oars back. Just one more stroke and she would be there. Lobster leapt high into the air and dived down into the water. He swam against the current like a missile through the waves. He was by far the best swimmer and the right one for the job. Pip and Penelope held on to the remains of the soggy cigar box, but it would soon sink. Pip started to panic, waving his paws.

"Help!" cried Penelope. "My brother can't swim." She grabbed Pip by his little braces and held on to him for dear life.

The cigar box sank and Penelope couldn't hold on to Pip as the waves crashed over them.

Pip followed the cigar box deep down into the ocean.

Penelope scoured the surface of the water, but she couldn't see anything.

"Don't worry," called Emmeline. "Lobster will find him." She reached over, grabbed Penelope and pulled her to safety.

Poor Penelope sat shivering on Alice's lap, while Alice tried to warm her with her hands.

"Look!" shrieked Emmeline, pointing at the water.

"I can't see anything, my dear," said Starfish, scanning the surface.

"There, there," shouted Emmeline, as bubbles started to appear.

A couple more bubbles came up and then lots more ... and then up popped Pip's red hat, followed by Lobster, with Pip on his back.

"He saved me," gasped Pip.

The lobster swam around with pride and flipped Pip high into the air so he landed in the boat.

"Thank you, thank you." Emmeline wrung Pip's hat out and placed it back on his head.

"Now can we have lunch?"

Everyone turned to look at Chesterpuss.

"What?" said Chesterpuss, looking surprised.

"All you ever think about is your stomach." Emmeline narrowed her eyes at her rude cat.

"I don't get to look this good without eating every couple of hours," said Chesterpuss. "If I don't eat soon, I may have to make do with lobster tail or a crab claw," he added, eyeing up the lobster.

Starfish stood in the middle of the boat, among Lobster, Crab and Chesterpuss. "We are not going to eat each other," she said, waving her seven gloves around and pointing them at Chesterpuss. "We will head back to shore and make our way back home for lunch."

"She's right," said Emmeline, looking at Alice, who was still holding Penelope in her lap. "Alice needs food too, to keep her strength up."

Emmeline picked up the oars and paddled back to the shore.

Chapter 8
The Pine Forest

It was hard work walking through the sand – especially the soft white kind. Pip and Penelope were nestled in the pocket of Alice's cardigan. Pip had fallen asleep and was bobbing up and down to the rhythm of Alice's walking. Chesterpuss was leading the way, followed by Lobster, Crab and Starfish.

They reached the edge of the forest and there on the white beach, surrounded by pine trees, was the biggest clam shell Alice had ever seen. In the centre was a door with a big yellow handle.

"Wow, it's incredible. Is this your home?" Alice asked the starfish.

"Yes, it's our home." Starfish smiled.

One by one they entered the shell, and a lovely smell hit their noses.

"Mmmm... smells like fish stew," said Chesterpuss

"That will be Moonface, cooking up a storm," said Crab.

"And only the best fish stew," said Starfish.

They went along the corridor, which was so beautifully smooth and opalescent that you could almost see your reflection in it.

"What an adventure," said Alice. "It's like being in a story book," she whispered to Emmeline.

They walked along several corridors and through a number of doors before they came to a bright yellow door. Surely this had to be the last one, thought Alice. Starfish opened the door – and there to greet them was a strange-looking man. Alice stared across at him through the steamy room. He was stirring a very large pot of fish stew.

The man looked up and greeted everyone with a big smile. He had bulbous cheeks, big eyes and long curly hair. *Maybe he was some kind of troll*, thought Alice.

"This is Moonface," said Starfish, pulling out chairs for everyone to sit down.

Pip yawned, stretched his little arms and reached up to peep out of Alice's pocket. "Something smells good," he said, looking around for Penelope, who was sitting on the table next to Emmeline.

Moonface tipped the stew into a jug and poured a little into each bowl on the table.

"I'm so hungry," said Alice, who was starting to look very tired after all the excitement.

"Me too," piped up Chesterpuss, lapping up the fish stew as though it was his last meal.

Alice whispered to Emmeline, "Why doesn't Moonface talk?"

"He hasn't spoken since he lost his dear friend, Moonpie. She was taken by the evil sand warlock," said Emmeline.

"Sand warlock?" said Alice.

"Yes," said Starfish. "We found Moonface wandering through the pine forest. Lost, he was, and very sad."

"We took him in and gave him a home," said Lobster.

"We believe his friend is a prisoner of the sand warlock," said Starfish. "He takes people prisoner and drags them down below the sand, never to be seen again."

"We must do something," said Alice. "I know what it's like to be a prisoner." She gave a sob. "My mother has kept me in my bedroom for years, until today. But now I feel alive, thanks to my cousin here. Emmeline," she went on, "we must do something to help Moonface get his friend back."

"I can't bear to think of Moonpie all alone," said Moonface.

Everyone looked up in surprise, as it was the first time Moonface had spoken in a very long time.

"Lobster, there must be something we can do," said Alice.

"The sand warlock will just turn us all to sand, once he has extracted all our wishes," replied Lobster.

"That's what he'll do, like he has always done," agreed Crab.

"Once he's taken your wishes away, all you've ever dreamed of will be gone for good," said Chesterpuss. "Like days full of porridge and tuna."

"And a whole mountain of cheese to eat your way through," said Pip.

"And a lifetime of fish stew," said Moonface.

"We can't just sit here and do nothing," cried Alice. "He has to be stopped." She looked at Chesterpuss, who was now full of fish stew, for back-up.

Chesterpuss let out a great big burp. "Much better," he said.

"OK, I'm in," said Lobster.

Chesterpuss looked at Lobster. "I'm in too," he said, wanting to look as brave as Lobster.

Alice looked at Emmeline, Starfish and Crab, and then at Moonface. They all nodded.

"Good." Alice gave a squeal. "What an adventure!"

"We must leave this until morning," said Emmeline, looking at her watch. "We need to get back to the beach hut, otherwise nobody will be going anywhere." She thanked Starfish for lunch. "Here you are," she said, "have these as a thank you – you can have them for supper." She handed the jam tarts and sandwiches over.

Pip and Penelope jumped back into Alice's cardigan pocket as they all waved goodbye to their new friends. Back in the paddling boat, Emmeline rowed her way safely round the big pointy rock to the other side of the bay, where, standing proud, was the beach hut, now surrounded by a very bright orange light.

"Come quick," said Chesterpuss, running towards the hut.

"It's ready to fly," shrieked Emmeline, grabbing Alice by the hand and pulling her along. They all ran as fast as they could. Pip and Penelope bounced up and down, up and down, inside the cardigan pocket.

Chesterpuss reached the hut first and pushed the door open, followed by Emmeline, who flung herself over the doorstep and landed on the wicker chair. She was followed by Alice. The door slammed shut and Emmeline placed her finger on the map – on the village of Blakeney.

The hut began to vibrate, then from side to side it rocked and *whoosh!* – into the air it went. Chesterpuss clung to his cushion and Emmeline clung to Alice. Pip and Penelope popped their heads out of Alice's pocket and Pip pulled his hat over his ears. The shutters on the window clattered and banged and the wind rushed around the beach hut. Debris flew by the window – sticks and litter and a big rubbish bin. The weather changed from sunshine to rain and then snow. And finally, with an almighty *whizz, bang!* – down it came with a thud.

They had landed safely, back in the garden in Blakeney village.

"Are we here?" said Penelope.

"Yes, we're back," said Emmeline.

Chesterpuss did a roly-poly and sat upright. "Time for tea," he said, heading for the door.

"Er, wait a moment," said Emmeline. "I need you to fetch Mr James for me, so we can get Alice back to her room without Aunt Adna seeing her."

The time was 3.55 pm and they had only five minutes before Aunt Adna returned. Mr James slammed Alice's door shut just in time, as Adna reached the top of the stairs.

"What is wrong, Mr James? And can you stop slamming doors?" said Adna.

"Nothing, Lady Adna. I was just ... just bringing Alice a drink," he said nervously.

"Please can you get out of my way – I wish to see my daughter."

Mr James moved away from the door.

Alice was tucked up in bed, feeling very happy with how her day had gone.

Adna reached over and felt her daughter's forehead. "You have a temperature, my dear, and you look all flushed," she said.

"I'm fine, mother – please stop fussing," Alice said.

"I'm not fussing. I will ask Nancy to bring you some medicine up." With that, Adna left the room.

Adna rang her bell and Nancy came running. "Could you please run a bath for Alice and bring her medicine?" Adna asked.

Nancy did as she was told.

The water ran warm across Alice's body as she closed her eyes and thought about the day she'd had. And, most important of all, what tomorrow would bring for everyone.

Someone knocked on the door. Alice grabbed her dressing gown as Emmeline entered the bathroom.

"The plan for tomorrow is to set off about 9 am, just after your mother has left," whispered Emmeline. "And I've asked Nancy to make us another picnic. Pip and Penelope are staying in my bedroom tonight and I'm going to find them another box to sleep in."

Suddenly they heard a noise on the stairs.

"Quickly, you must go," said Alice. "That will be Mother." She pushed Emmeline out of the bathroom and shut the door.

"Into bed now," said Adna to Alice. "And get some sleep – you need your sleep."

"Yes, I do need my sleep," said Alice, with a smile on her face. She couldn't wait for morning – if only her mother knew.

Chapter 9
Back to the Beach

Emmeline opened her curtains and the sun shone through. The garden looked so much more inviting now the beach hut was in it.

A long beam of sunlight hit Pip straight in the eye, making him squint and pull his hat over his eyes. Emmeline had made the mice a makeshift bed out of an empty shoe box, in which there was room for at least ten mice. She had given them a pretty embroidered hanky to sleep under.

"Morning, did you sleep well?" she asked them.

"Yes, thank you," squeaked Penelope.

"Hop into my pocket – it's time for breakfast." Emmeline was raring to go to the beach hut. She had hardly slept, knowing what today was going to bring.

In the kitchen, Nancy was frying the bacon and Chesterpuss sat watching, in the hope that something might fall his way. Mr James was whistling his favourite tune: *Oh when the saints go marching in, oh when the saints go marching in ...*

Chesterpuss sighed – he had heard enough – and jumped up onto the table.

"Get down," Mr James bellowed.

"Can anyone get any breakfast around here?" said a very hungry Chesterpuss.

"Get off my table!" The sweeping brush knocked Chesterpuss off the table and across the kitchen. Nancy had a very good aim.

Mr James mashed up some porridge and tuna and placed the bowl down on the floor. Chesterpuss devoured the whole lot.

Nancy cracked the eggs over the frying pan – six in total, two each for Mr James and Adna and one each for Emmeline and Alice. The kettle on the Aga started to whistle and Mr James grabbed it just in time, before it boiled over. The eggs were done, the bacon was crispy and the bread and tea were ready. Nancy loaded everything onto her trolley and wheeled it to the dining room.

She knocked, as she always did, and Adna shouted, "Enter."

"I hope you're all hungry," said Nancy.

There in the dining room were Adna, Emmeline and Alice. Alice had persuaded her mother to allow her downstairs instead of eating her breakfast in bed as usual.

"Thank you, Nancy," said Adna.

Nancy had noticed that Adna's mood seemed to be changing. In fact, everyone's mood was so much brighter since Emmeline and her beach hut had arrived. Alice no longer looked like a sick child with a face like a white ghost. She now had glowing red cheeks and she wore bright-coloured clothing which complemented her long, blond curly hair. Aunt Adna had even let Chesterpuss into the dining room and was feeding him sardines.

"I have allowed Emmeline to take Alice down to her beach hut for a picnic today," Adna said to Nancy. "Please ensure she is safe while I'm away."

"I promise I'll look after her," said Nancy, winking at Alice.

Aunt Adna finished her breakfast and patted Chesterpuss on the head. "Such a marvellous pussy you are," she said, stuffing another sardine into Chesterpuss's mouth.

Chesterpuss began to purr, in between mouthfuls of fish.

"Isn't it such a glorious day today?" continued Aunt Adna.

Alice looked at her mother and liked what she saw – a beautiful, happy lady. Aunt Adna kissed her daughter on the cheek and said goodbye for the day.

Nancy came back to collect the breakfast plates. "Have you finished?" she asked Emmeline.

"Yes, thank you," said Emmeline trying to push Pip back down into her pocket. She had put a rather large piece of toast in there for Pip and Penelope to munch on for their breakfast. She didn't want Nancy to see the mice or it would be bedlam. Nancy hated mice.

"I've made you a picnic for today – come and collect it when you're ready." Nancy wheeled her trolley away with the breakfast plates on it.

Excited by the journey ahead, Alice and Emmeline skipped along to the kitchen.

"There you go," said Nancy, stuffing extra jam tarts into their basket. "Be back for 4pm." She waved them off as they walked down the garden path.

Pip had found a piece of wool inside Emmeline's pocket. The wool was getting longer and longer, creating a hole in Emmeline's cardigan. Eventually Pip and Penelope could see the ground and Emmeline's shoes. They clung to the piece of wool as they fell out of the hole. The ground got closer and closer and then Pip and Penelope *boinged* back up as though on a piece of elastic ... and then back down again, just missing the ground.

They were both swinging left and right as Emmeline, unaware, carried on towards the beach hut, passing the fountain with its silver water sprinkling down into a small pool.

"Emmeline!" shouted Pip. It was no good – Emmeline couldn't hear Pip and Penelope as she skipped along with Alice. They skipped through the arch and there it was – her lovely green and cream beach hut.

Chesterpuss had beaten them to it and was already sitting in the doorway. He watched Emmeline skipping up to the door and something caught his eye. It was Pip and Penelope, swinging from side to side, clinging on for dear life. Suddenly the mice were flung straight at Chesterpuss and hit him bang on the nose.

"Meoooooowwwww!" screeched Chesterpuss. He grabbed Pip and Penelope and pulled them to the ground. This was like a game to Chesterpuss as he went to swipe them with his paw – and then he remembered his promise not to hurt the mice.

Emmeline pulled the piece of wool from her cardigan, picked up the mice and wagged her finger at Chesterpuss in a disapproving way. Chesterpuss sat himself down on his cushion. Alice sat on the little wicker chair and

Emmeline sat down on another cushion – all waiting for the beach hut to fly.

"Look!" Penelope squealed with excitement. "We have a new bed." And there it was – a wooden cigar box all painted in a pretty green colour. Penelope slid the box open and inside was a little bed, ready-made for them. It looked so welcoming that Pip and Penelope jumped straight in.

"Time for the countdown," called Emmeline, pointing her finger at Holkham on the map.

The hut vibrated and shook.

"Hold on, everyone," called out Alice.

The beach hut lifted into the air and spun round and round. The wind whistled around the window and the shutters sprang open. The noise was so loud that Alice covered her ears. The cigar box slid along the shelf, tipped over the edge and descended towards the ground. Chesterpuss sprang into the air and, before the box hit the floor, caught it in his paws.

"Well done," shouted Emmeline over the noise.

The hut suddenly let out a *whizz* and a *whoosh* – and landed with a big thud.

"You absolutely wonderful cat," Emmeline said, patting and kissing Chesterpuss on the head.

"Stop the kissing," Chesterpuss said, opening the cigar box to see if Pip and Penelope were all right.

Out they popped, looking a little shaken. Pip adjusted his red hat and Penelope straightened her dress.

"That was some ride," said Pip.

"We're here," said Alice, pushing the door open onto the most glorious white sand. The sun was beating down and seagulls were flying around in the sky. Out of the corner of one eye, Chesterpuss watched a seagull as it came swooping down towards Pip and Penelope. Chesterpuss jumped at the seagull and managed to scare it away.

"You've become quite a hero," said Emmeline, patting Chesterpuss again on the head.

"I think it would be a good idea to travel in my pocket like before," said Alice to the mice. They agreed it would be a lot safer in Alice's pocket.

"Look!" shouted Emmeline, pointing out to sea.

"It's Lobster, Starfish, Crab and Moonface," Alice said, waving frantically and running down to the sea to meet them.

Alice helped to pull the boat ashore.

"Well, are we all ready?" said Lobster, taking the lead as usual.

"I think I should lead this army," said Chesterpuss, puffing out his chest. "After all, I've completed two rescue missions already this morning," he added, with a big grin on his face.

"I don't believe it," said the lobster.

"For heaven's sake, you two," said Emmeline, bursting into laughter.

Alice, Pip and Penelope joined in and soon they were all rolling around in the sand.

"What about me leading the way?" came the quiet voice of Moonface.

"Hear, hear!" said everyone.

"As long as we all stay together and head towards the circle marked in the sand," said Moonface.

"I've heard he will turn you into seaweed," said Crab.

"And boil you up as stew," said Lobster.

"Then we must all stay together," said Emmeline.

Moonface led the way as they walked across the sand towards the edge of the forest. It felt as though they had been walking for hours when Moonface stopped. "You see that huge pine tree ahead of us, just next to the sand dune?" he whispered.

"I see it," said Emmeline.

They all peered through the trees at the largest pine tree.

"That's where the circle in the sand is – and where I last saw Moonpie," said Moonface.

"Do you think we should sneak up or make a full run up to it?" said Alice, feeling the excitement grow.

"I think we should sneak up," said Chesterpuss.

"Then let's go," said Lobster.

As they approached the big pine tree, they heard something rustle and they all stopped in their tracks. They stood like statues and waited for something to happen.

Chapter 10
The Sand Warlock

The sand stirred and shifted, and ripples crept along it to Moonface's feet.

"What on earth is it?" said Emmeline.

"It's him – it's the sand warlock." Moonface was shaking with fear.

"I'm not afraid," said Chesterpuss, pushing himself forward, followed by Lobster not far behind.

"Come out and show yourself to us," boomed Chesterpuss.

"Leave me alone!" said a voice, deep down in the sand. "I want to sleep," came the voice again.

"He wants to sleep?" said Alice.

Suddenly a hole appeared in the sand and they all stood back.

"Why do you disturb me?" The voice became louder.

"We've come to rescue our friend Moonpie," shouted Moonface.

They all stood back as sand shot into the air, followed by a brown furry creature who landed right in front of Chesterpuss.

"What is it?" shrieked Alice.

"Is it a teddy bear?" said Pip, popping out of Emmeline's pocket.

The thing yawned and opened its eyes.

"Don't look," Starfish cried. "Cover your eyes or he'll take your wishes away."

"What utter nonsense you speak," the thing said, and yawned.

"So you don't take people's wishes away?" said Chesterpuss, uncovering his eyes.

"Don't be ridiculous." The thing shuffled forward, and they all stepped back. The thing spotted Emmeline with the picnic basket. "What do you have in there? I'm rather hungry after sleeping for a whole year." He peered over the rim of the basket.

"Shall we take him home with us?" Alice said. "He is rather cute."

"No, we can't take him home – and will you get out of my basket?" Emmeline grabbed the thing, who was now covered in jam tarts.

"He's like a Tasmanian devil," said Chesterpuss.

"How rude. I'm not a devil, I'm a bunglephant," the thing said, licking his lips.

"So you're not a sand warlock and you don't take people's wishes away?" said Emmeline.

"No and no – and I don't have your friend. Moonpie is safe and sound."

They all listened to the bunglephant with great interest.

"Come close and gather round," he said to Emmeline.

They gathered round and Bunglephant drew a square in the sand. The sand dissolved and a glass window appeared. They bent over the window and stared down – and there was Moonpie, laughing and jumping high into the sky. She was surrounded by her family, living deep in the forest.

Moonface smiled to know his friend was happy and safe. The window disappeared and the sand spread quickly over the square.

"You see, she is fine – she was never taken by any sand warlock." The bunglephant yawned and rubbed his eyes. "Now if you don't mind, I need to sleep." With that, he jumped back into the hole and bade them all goodbye.

The sand spread and shuffled, and Bunglephant was gone.

"Well, I say we eat this picnic," said Chesterpuss.

So they all sat round and shared out the sandwiches and jam tarts, and Chesterpuss ate his tuna porridge. Pip and Penelope joined in, eating cheese sandwiches.

"Time to head back to the beach hut," said Emmeline, helping Alice pack up the picnic basket.

By the time they had reached the hut it was nearly 4 o'clock. Moonface, Lobster, Starfish and Crab waved goodbye to their friends as the beach hut took off.

"Bye!" shouted Alice.

High into the sky it went, higher and higher. Alice and Emmeline clung to the sides of the hut and Pip and Penelope nestled between Chesterpuss and his cushion.

Whizz! Bang! Whizz! Down it came with a thud. Pip and Penelope flew through the air like Frisbees™. Emmeline stretched out her hands and caught the mice in mid-flight. Chesterpuss was in his usual position, upside-down, and Alice was clinging to the cushion.

"What fun!" Alice said.

Emmeline jumped up and dashed out of the beach hut. "Come on," she shouted, running as quickly as she could down the garden path.

Pip and Penelope, now back in Emmeline's cardigan pocket, bounced up and down as she raced to the front door of the house. Alice and Chesterpuss followed, reaching the front door just as Aunt Adna came whistling through the garden gate.

Alice and Emmeline sat quickly down on the settee in the lounge, while Chesterpuss made his way to the kitchen to catch up with Mr James and Nancy.

The door opened and in walked Aunt Adna. "Hello girls. What a lovely day it has been." She kissed Emmeline on the cheek and then kissed Alice and gave her a big hug.

"You are looking so well, my darling," said Aunt Adna to Alice. "I have a little surprise for you." She pulled out a letter from her pocket. "It says you've been accepted for school in September." She smiled at her daughter and stroked her hair.

"How wonderful – you mean I can be like every other child and go to school?" said Alice, with tears of joy rolling down her cheeks.

Emmeline hugged Alice and looked across at her aunt. She was no longer spiky and stern; she had become the prettiest lady Emmeline had ever seen.

Across the room behind the big clock, Pip and Penelope looked on. Pip winked at Emmeline. In the kitchen, Nancy was singing along with Mr James and Chesterpuss was tucking into his favourite porridge and tuna. And at the bottom of the garden, a bright orange light shone around the beach hut, as the sun went down and the garden went to sleep.

Emmeline closed the curtains on another successful journey.

The End

Thank you for taking the time to read this book. If you enjoyed it, please consider telling your friends or posting a short review. Word of mouth is an author's best friend and much appreciated.

About the Author

Suzanne King loves to read children's books. Her favourite books are *The Lion The Witch and Wardrobe, Mary Poppins, Charlotte's Web* and *Chitty Chitty Bang Bang*, to name just a few. Suzanne loves the seaside and spending time walking along the beach.

https://www.facebook.com/charlottenocton/?pnref =story
https://www.smashwords.com/profile/view/charlotten octon
Twitter: https://twitter.com/elliot19cerys

http://crimsoncloakpublishing.com

Check out our children's corner

58352376R00054

Made in the USA
Charleston, SC
09 July 2016